Andy Russell,

NOT Wanted by the Police

Leach Library
276 Mammoth Road
Londonderry, NH 03053

Adult Services 432-1132
Children's Services 432-1127

Also by David A. Adler

**The Many Troubles
of Andy Russell**

Andy and Tamika

**School Trouble
for Andy Russell**

**Parachuting Hamsters
and Andy Russell**

Andy Russell,

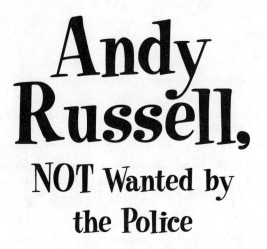

NOT Wanted by the Police

David A. Adler

With illustrations by
Leanne Franson

Gulliver Books • Harcourt, Inc.
San Diego   New York   London

For Deborah,
welcome to our family

www.harcourt.com

Gulliver Books is a trademark of Harcourt, Inc.,
registered in the United States of America and other jurisdictions.

Library of Congress Cataloging-in-Publication Data
Adler, David A.
Andy Russell, NOT wanted by the police / David A. Adler; with illustrations
by Leanne Franson.
p.   cm.
"Gulliver Books."
Summary: Andy and Tamika are watching their neighbor's house while they
are away, but when strange and troubling things start happening inside
the house, the police do not believe the children.
[1. Mystery and detective stories. 2. Neighbors—Fiction. 3. Schools—
Fiction.] I. Franson, Leanne, ill.   II. Title.
PZ7.A2615Ap   2001
[Fic]—dc21   2001001888
ISBN 0-15-216474-X

Text set in Century Old Style
Designed by Kaelin Chappell

First edition

A C E G H F D B

Printed in the United States of America

Contents

Chapter 1. Something Really Strange 1

Chapter 2. Armed and Dangerous 8

Chapter 3. The Mysterious Light 18

Chapter 4. Don't Turn Off That Light! 27

Chapter 5. Andy and the Police 34

Chapter 6. Stacy Ann's Great Idea 40

Chapter 7. I'll Scare Him Out 49

Chapter 8. LOOK! LOOK! 56

Chapter 9. Trapped in School 67

Chapter 10. I'm a Criminal 75

Chapter 11. ROAR! 80

Chapter 12. There's Someone in There 88

Chapter 13. Elke Bell 96

Chapter 14. A Really Good Day 110

Chapter 1
Something Really Strange

L ook what just came," Tamika Anderson told her friend Andy Russell. "It's a letter from the Perlmans. They're in Cotacachi."

Tamika started to read from it. " 'Dear Tamika.' "

Andy interrupted her. He smiled and said, "Cotacachi. That must be near Cognito. Lots of people go there, you know. People are always in Cognito."

"*Incognito* is a word, not a place," Tamika told

him. "When someone is *incognito* it means he's trying to keep people from knowing who he is."

"Oh," Andy said. "Is *that* what it means."

"Yes," Tamika said. " 'Dear Tamika,' " she read again.

"Maybe the Perlmans are near Clined," Andy said, "or Telligent. I think there's a big hill in Clined and an amusement park in Telligent, with a great roller coaster. People say it's good to be in Telligent. I think that's because of the roller coaster."

Tamika laughed. She rolled her eyes and said, "You know the Perlmans are in South America. Cotacachi is in Ecuador. It's near Otavalo."

"Oh," Andy said, and smiled.

" 'Dear Tamika,' " Tamika read again. She waited. When Andy didn't interrupt her, she went on. " 'We really miss you. We hope your parents are continuing to get better and that you are having fun staying with the Russells. Thanks so much for taking care of our house. And please, thank your friend Andy, too.' "

"They said you should thank me?" Andy asked.

"That's what it says here," Tamika answered. Then she read some more. " 'We're doing lots of research and lots of sight-seeing. Cotacachi is beautiful. It's lush and green. There are plants growing here that I have not seen anywhere else. Market day is fun. We've met lots of interesting people here and made some friends. We're buying interesting souvenirs. We miss you. Love, Miriam and Jonathan.' Then they wrote, 'P.S. There's a big surprise coming to you from South America.' "

"A surprise," Andy said. "Maybe she sent us turtles or iguanas or geckos. The Galapagos Islands are in Ecuador and they're famous for their animals."

"Whatever it is, I hope it gets here soon," Tamika said.

"Pirates once lived on the Galapagos," Andy said. "Maybe the Perlmans sent us lots of ancient gold coins or ancient pirates' eye-patches and wooden legs."

Andy put his hand over one eye and hopped around. "Ho, ho, ho," he said, "and a bottle of orange soda."

Tamika put the letter in her pocket. She tugged on Andy's shirt and said, "Come on, Captain Andy. Let's check on the Perlmans' house."

The Perlmans' house is next door to the Russells'. Tamika had lived with the Perlmans for a year, while her parents were recovering from a car accident. Then the Perlmans left to travel to South America for their work, and Tamika moved in with the Russells. She shared a room with Rachel, Andy's older sister.

Andy and Tamika were in the Russells' kitchen. Andy hopped to the cabinet under the sink and took out a large black plastic bag. "Let's fill their outside garbage can again, so if a thieving pirate looks, he'll think someone is home."

Andy took the lid off the kitchen trash can, reached in, and took out an apple core. He put it in the bag and said, "This is all there was in there. We've got to get more stuff."

The basement can was empty. Andy found some tissues in the bathroom wastebasket and dumped them into the bag. Upstairs, on his desk, he found some old tests and school papers. "This stuff is *real* junk," he told Tamika as he threw the papers into the bag.

Next they went into Tamika and Rachel's room. Rachel was sitting at her desk, writing. Andy held

the black plastic bag open. "Hop in," he told Rachel.

"I'm busy. I'm doing homework."

"And I'm collecting garbage." He took Rachel's pillow, her pajamas, and some papers from her desk and said, "Thank you."

Rachel grabbed her things. "Get out," she told Andy. "And Tamika, you should find some less annoying friends."

Mrs. Russell, who taught math at the local high school, was in her room, sitting at her desk and grading test papers. She gave Andy the morning newspaper to add to his garbage collection.

"Maybe we'll find some things outside," Tamika said, "some supermarket flyers, or papers that blew into the yard."

There were no papers in the front or back yards of the Russell or Perlman houses.

"Hey," Andy said. "I just thought of something. Why don't we take the stuff from our outdoor garbage cans and put it in the Perlmans'?"

Andy took the lids off his family's two trash cans. They were both empty.

"Just our luck," Andy said. "Today must have

been pick-up day." He shook the almost empty plastic bag he was holding and said, "I'll just put this in the Perlmans' trash can. It's better than nothing."

They walked across the Perlmans' driveway and around to the back of the house. Andy took the lid off the garbage can.

"WHAT!" Andy shouted. "What's this?"

Tamika looked in. "It's garbage," she said.

"I know what it is, but what's it doing here?" Andy took out an empty Oat Bran Toasties cereal box. "We don't eat this stuff, and even if we did, the garbage was collected today."

Tamika's eyes widened. "Someone else must have put that in there," she said. "But Miriam told me we're the only ones watching the house."

"There's something strange going on here," Andy said, and shook the Oat Bran Toasties box. "Something *really* strange."

Chapter 2
Armed and Dangerous

I know what's going on," Andy said. "There was a thieving pirate in the house. He stole the Perlmans' books and vases and pictures and menorah and barber's chair and everything!"

"Something strange *is* going on," Tamika replied. "But I don't think there's a thief in the house."

"You don't?"

"Think about it," Tamika said. "Would someone break into the house and steal everything and then sit down and eat breakfast? The Perlmans don't eat Oat Bran Toasties, so if you're right, the thief brought it, and after he was done, he took out the garbage."

"Yeah," Andy admitted. "That doesn't make sense."

"But you're right about one thing. Something strange *is* going on here, and we should find out what it is."

Andy looked at the cereal box he was holding. He thought for a moment. Then he took the lid off the can again and looked in.

"Do you know what's in here?" he asked.

"Garbage?"

"No. Clues. Look at all that stuff. Each piece of garbage is like a fingerprint. All we have to do is study this stuff, and we'll learn a lot about whoever put it in here."

Tamika leaned over the can. "These sure are smelly clues."

Andy took out an empty bag of ginger-snap cookies, an empty skim-milk container, some used green-tea bags, one large worn army boot, and a *Power Spider* comic book.

"Green tea and skim milk," Tamika said. "It's

health-nut stuff! But why would a health nut throw out just one boot?"

"He's a thieving one-legged pirate. That's why," Andy said. "But why would anyone read *Power Spider*? It's got lousy stories."

Andy took the now almost empty plastic bag out of the garbage can. He rolled up his sleeve and reached deep into the bag.

"Yuck!" he said, and took out some cantaloupe rind.

"Here, try this," Tamika told him. She took the bag from Andy and turned it upside down. More cantaloupe rinds, some cantaloupe seeds, a torn T-shirt, an apple core, dirty paper cups and paper napkins, two paintbrushes, a squeezed-out tube of paint, crumpled tissues, and a woman's purple stocking fell out.

Andy and Tamika studied the garbage.

"There's a man's army boot and a woman's purple stocking," Andy noted. "I'm getting a weird picture in my head of whoever threw this stuff out. Maybe he really *is* a pirate."

"And look at all those tissues," Tamika said. "He probably has a cold."

"Or an allergy," Andy added. "The Perlmans

have been away for two months. The house must be real dusty. Lots of people are allergic to dust. It makes them sneeze."

With her foot, Tamika turned over the T-shirt and paint tubes. She kicked some of the tissues. Then she told Andy, "I think we should put everything back into the bag."

Andy reached down.

"EW! Don't use your hands," Tamika told him. "That stuff must be covered with germs."

"Germs and DNA," Andy said. "I bet if we took this stuff to a lab, a scientist could make a clone of whoever threw this stuff out."

"Great," Tamika said, "two one-legged pirates. That's just what we need hopping around."

Andy tore the Oat Bran Toasties box into a makeshift cardboard shovel. He used it to clean up the mess. When he was done, Tamika said, "Maybe we should walk around the house to see if anything else looks suspicious."

"Aha!" Andy said. "You *do* think there may be a thief. And I think we should be real careful. Someone who breaks into houses might be armed and dangerous."

"I *don't* think someone broke in. I just want to be sure. We'll walk around quietly and look at all the windows and doors, make sure they're closed."

Tamika started toward the back door and Andy pulled on her sleeve. "Maybe we should call the police," he whispered.

"And what would we tell them?" Tamika asked. "That we found garbage in the Perlmans' trash cans?"

Andy and Tamika walked along the edge of the yard, far away from the house. The windows in the back of the house were all closed. The shades were down.

"We should try the back door," Tamika whispered.

"It's closed," Andy said.

"I know that," Tamika said. "But one of us should check if it's still locked."

Tamika walked slowly toward the back door. Andy followed her. Tamika quietly tried the back door.

"Good." Tamika sighed. The door was locked, just the way the Perlmans had left it.

Andy and Tamika hurried to the back edge of the yard again. They quietly walked to the side of the house. The windows there were closed, too, but some of the shades were up.

"I'm not sure," Tamika whispered, "but I think Miriam had pulled all the shades down."

Andy walked very slowly to one of the windows with a shade that was up. He got up on his toes and looked in.

"Yikes!" Andy gasped and dropped to the ground. "There's someone in there!"

Andy and Tamika waited, scared to move.

"I don't hear anyone moving around in there," Tamika finally whispered.

She got on her toes and looked in, then laughed.

"You were looking at yourself!" Tamika told Andy. "You scared yourself. There's a mirror in the study, and that's what you saw."

"I did?" Andy asked. He looked through the window again. He saw his reflection in the study mirror. "Oh, I did," he said.

Tamika looked at the room for a long time. Then she told Andy, "Everything is just the way I remember it. The barber's chair is still there, and all the books and the menorah are there, too."

They walked to the front of the house. Andy ran to the front door, tried it, and ran back to Tamika. "It's locked, too," he told her.

The windows on the other side of the house were all closed. The shades there were down. They hurried to the Russells' backyard.

"What do we do now?" Andy asked.

Tamika shook her head and said, "I don't know. At first I thought all this garbage stuff was silly, but now I think it's spooky."

Andy turned and looked at the Perlmans' house. Then he smiled and said, "If we go to the police, I could describe the thief. One of their artists could sketch a picture of him. He's a one-legged man wearing one large boot and a purple stocking. And he drinks skim milk and green tea, so he's probably skinny."

Tamika laughed and added, "And he has a long scraggly beard and an eye patch."

"That garbage taught us a lot," Andy said. "You know, it's a key to our identity. It really is. And guess what I just thought of—a great idea for a new TV game show! There would be people and piles of garbage, and contestants would have to match the people to their garbage. It would be lots of fun. They could ask the people questions—not what they eat but maybe what their jobs are and things like that."

"And the grand prize," Tamika said, "could be a year's supply of garbage bags."

"Yeah."

"Now, let's get back to the Perlmans' house," Tamika said. "What are we going to do?"

"Maybe we should tell my parents," Andy suggested. "And we should watch the house day and night. We could take turns, like real detectives."

Andy lifted his hands, bent his fingers in what he thought was a spooky way, and said, "This will be a stakeout."

"We *should* tell your parents," Tamika said.

"And I think we should watch the house. The window in my room faces it. We should take turns looking out, probably even late at night. That's when there's real trouble. That's when thieves do most of their work."

"OK," Tamika agreed. "We'll tell your parents

what we found, and then we'll take turns watching the house."

Andy said, "I hope we really find a one-legged man wearing one purple stocking."

"And I hope we don't," Tamika told him. "I don't want anyone spooking around next door. I hope no one went into the house."

Chapter 3
The Mysterious Light

I s that you?" Rachel called as Andy and Tamika entered the house.

"Who?" Andy asked.

"You," Rachel answered, and hurried down the steps. "I have to talk to you."

"And we have to talk to Mom and Dad," Andy told her.

"It's important," Tamika added.

"This is important, too. I didn't know what to do for the science fair and Ms. Jackson, my teacher, had a great idea. She said I should test Andy's gerbils and see which one is the smartest."

"Where are Mom and Dad?" Andy asked.

"Dad said he'll make a maze. I'll make tags and you could put them on the gerbils, on their tails or maybe on their feet. Then I'll time them through the maze. I'll see if one always gets through the fastest."

Rachel followed Andy and Tamika as they walked through the kitchen, dining room, and living room.

"Where are they?" Andy asked. "Where are Mom and Dad?"

"So, will you let me?" Rachel asked. "Will you let me use your gerbils?"

"Listen," Tamika told Rachel, "we have to find your parents. We have to tell them about what we found at the Perlmans'."

"If I tell you where they are, will you let me use your gerbils?"

"Mom! Dad!" Andy called as he pushed past his sister.

Rachel followed Andy and Tamika upstairs. The Russells weren't in their bedroom.

Then they heard some banging.

"Mom! Dad!" Andy called again. "Are you in the attic?"

"We're up here," Mr. Russell answered.

Andy opened the door to his mother's closet and looked up. The hatchway to the attic was open and a rope ladder was hanging down.

Andy held on to the two sides of the ladder. "I'm coming up," he announced.

"We're all coming up," Tamika said.

Andy slowly climbed the shaky rope ladder. When his head was through the hatch, he held on to the sides of the hatchway and pulled himself into the attic.

Mr. Russell had cut a hole in the roof and built a dormer. Mrs. Russell was holding a window frame while Mr. Russell nailed it in.

"Please," Mrs. Russell said, "hold this for Dad."

Mrs. Russell was pregnant. The baby was expected in a few months, and Mr. Russell hoped to have the room he was building in the attic ready by then. Andy hoped the baby would take his room, so he could move into the big attic room. He thought it would be great to have an entire floor to himself.

Andy held on to the window frame while his father knocked in more nails.

Hurry, Andy thought. He was anxious to tell his parents about the Perlmans' house.

Tamika was the next to go up the rope ladder. Then Rachel went up. Rachel tried to shout over her dad's hammering, but no one heard her. Finally, Mr. Russell was done.

"You have to tell Andy to let me test his gerbils," Rachel said.

"Mom, Dad," Andy said, while Rachel was still talking, "Tamika and I have to talk to you. Something strange is going on at the Perlmans' house, and we don't know what to do."

"One at a time," Mrs. Russell told them.

"I'm the oldest. I'll go first," Rachel said quickly. "And all I need is for you to tell Andy to let me test his gerbils. I won't hurt them, and it's for school."

Mr. Russell put his hammer down. "What do you think?" he asked Andy. "She won't hurt the gerbils. It may even be fun for them."

Rachel said, "You'll put tags on the gerbils and put them in the maze."

"If I'm handling the gerbils and Dad is making the maze, what are *you* doing?"

"I'm making a chart and I'm timing the gerbils."

Andy folded his arms and looked at Rachel.

"The gerbils love to go through tunnels, so they'll love going through mazes, too," Rachel said. "And Dad is good at making wood stuff, so he'll make a great maze."

"OK," Andy said. "But only if the gerbils seem to like it."

"I'll help, too," Tamika added.

"Now, Mom and Dad," Andy said, "may I *please* tell you what's happening at the Perlmans'?"

He didn't wait for an answer. "We don't *know* what's happening," he said, and threw up his hands. "That's the problem! Someone put garbage in the Perlmans' garbage can. And it's strange stuff—a man's army boot, a woman's purple stocking, and green-tea bags. Who would drink green tea?"

"It's simple," Mr. Russell said calmly. "Someone else knows the Perlmans are away. He's also watching the house. It's probably one of the neighbors."

"But the Perlmans told me we were the only

22

ones watching the house," Tamika said. "And we've been watching it for a long time now, and this is the first time we've found someone else's garbage in the garbage can."

Mr. Russell put his hammer in the toolbox and said, "It is strange, but it's only garbage. I don't think it's anything to worry about. Just to be sure, though, we can all keep an eye on the house."

"That's right," Mrs. Russell said. "We'll all watch the house."

That afternoon Andy and Tamika did their homework by the window in Andy's room. They often looked out at the Perlmans' house, but they didn't see anything unusual.

After dinner Tamika watched the Perlmans' house and Andy watched TV. Tamika didn't see anything happening. Then it was Andy's turn to watch their house.

It was late. Most nights, by this time Andy was asleep. Andy changed into his pajamas. He stuffed a few pairs of pants and a volleyball under his pillow, to prop it up. He turned off the light in his room. Then he lay down on his bed and looked out the window.

OK, Mr. Thief, Andy said to himself, *I dare you*

to try something now with Detective Andy Russell on the case.

But Detective Andy Russell was tired. He was soon asleep.

A few hours later Andy turned onto his side. The volleyball rolled off the bed. The pillow dropped and the detective woke up.

"What happened?" Andy asked.

He looked out the window. There was a light on in the Perlmans' house, in the room Tamika used to sleep in, the room just opposite Andy's.

Hey, Andy thought, *that light wasn't on before.*

Andy hurried into the hall. He knocked on the door of Rachel and Tamika's room.

"What is it?" Rachel asked.

"There's a light on," Andy answered.

"Turn it off and go to sleep," Rachel told him.

"No. It's on in the Perlmans' house. Tamika, wake up."

Andy waited.

Rachel and Tamika came out of their room. Then Mr. Russell came out of his room.

"It's late. What are you doing up?" he asked.

Andy told him about the light.

Tamika, Rachel, and Mr. Russell followed Andy

into his room. Andy pointed out his window and said, "There's someone in that house. That light wasn't on before."

"And it's not on now," Rachel said.

Andy looked out his window. The light *wasn't* on!

"I think I need to test *your* intelligence," Rachel said, "not the gerbils'."

"It's late," Mr. Russell told everyone. "Go to sleep."

"I'm not crazy. I saw a light," Andy insisted.

"Sure you're crazy," Rachel said, and left Andy's room. Tamika and Mr. Russell left, too.

Andy imagined someone was looking out the now darkened Perlman window. Andy pointed and said, "I'll catch you. That's right. I will. No one-legged thief can hop fast enough to get away from Detective Andy Russell."

Chapter 4
Don't Turn Off That Light!

Maybe *someone there is watching me,* Andy thought. *Maybe Mr. Someone turned off the light when he saw me get help.*

Maybe Mr. Someone is a thief. Maybe he's in the living room right now, filling a large sack with the Perlmans' chess set and television.

"Put that television back," Andy Russell said.

Andy thought about Dr. Perlman's favorite chair, the old barber's chair he had in his study.

"Don't even think of stealing it," Andy said. "You'll never get it out the door."

Andy sat on his bed for a while. He looked out his window, to the Perlmans' house. He waited for something to happen. But nothing did.

I bet he's in his car now, about to make his getaway. But he won't, not with Detective Andy Russell on the case!

Andy got off his bed and quietly went into the hall. The door to Rachel and Tamika's room was closed. The door to his parents' room was closed, too. Andy quietly walked downstairs. He opened the front door and went outside.

There was no car parked in front of the Perlmans' house. There was no Mr. Someone dragging out Dr. Perlman's barber chair.

Andy realized he was outside with just his pajamas on. He looked up and down his block. The street was quiet. There was no one around to see him. Then he started down the path and realized he was barefoot, too. Walking on the stone path hurt his feet.

Andy stood on the sidewalk and looked across the Perlmans' lawn to their house. Their door was closed. All the lights in the front of the house were off. He slowly walked toward the Perlmans', then onto the lawn along one side of their house. Andy walked to the back and then along the other side of the house. All the inside lights were off, too.

It's spooky out here, Andy thought. *It's cold and windy, too.*

The shades in the rooms upstairs were up.

Maybe Mr. Someone is looking out and watching me!

Andy hurried home. He tried to turn the front-door knob, but he couldn't.

Oh no, Andy thought. *I locked myself out!*

Andy looked up. All the lights in his house were off, too.

He knocked on the door. No one answered. He knocked louder, and still no one opened the door.

Andy shivered. It was much too cold to be outside in just pajamas. And it was too dark.

Creak!

Andy heard a noise.

Creak!

He heard it again.

He's coming to get me, Andy thought.

He knocked on the door again.

Tamika and Rachel's room was right above him.

"Hey!" Andy called out. "Hey!" he called again, louder this time.

Andy waited, but no one came to the door.

Creak!

Andy turned. He didn't see anyone. He quickly found a few small rocks in the flower bed. He threw them, one at a time, at the window of Tamika and Rachel's room. The first rock didn't go high enough. The second one was too high. The third one hit the window.

Ping!

Andy waited. He expected the shade to go up. He expected Tamika or Rachel to look out the window. But nothing happened.

Creak!

Andy was really scared now. He got some more rocks from the flower bed—a few big ones and a handful of small ones. He carefully threw the big rocks, one at a time. The last one hit the middle of the window.

Ping!

"Come on!" Andy said.

When nothing happened, he threw the handful of small rocks. Lots of them hit the window.

"HEY!" Andy shouted. "LET ME IN!"

The light in Tamika and Rachel's room went on. The shade went up and Rachel opened the window.

"What are you doing out there?"

"Please, just open the door. Open it before he gets me."

Tamika came to the window.

"Come on," Andy said. "Hurry!"

More lights in the Russell house went on. Then the front door was opened. Tamika, Rachel, and Andy's parents were all there, looking at Andy.

"What are you doing outside?" Mr. Russell asked as Andy hurried inside.

"I think there's someone out there," Andy said.

Andy's parents looked outside.

Creak!

"Did you hear that? Did you hear that spooky creaking sound?"

"That's the wind," Mr. Russell said. "It's blowing the branches of one of the trees against the eaves of the house. It does that a lot."

"Well, it's spooky," Andy said. He was glad when his father closed the door.

Mrs. Russell asked again, "What were you doing outside?"

"I was checking on the Perlmans' house."

"I know why," Rachel said sarcastically. "He saw another light on next door and went over there to turn it off."

"No," Andy told her. "I didn't see any more lights."

"Did you find anything?" Tamika asked.

"No."

"I think it's time you went to bed," Mr. Russell said. "I think it's time we all went to bed. It's past midnight."

"I'm glad you looked. I'm worried, too," Tamika whispered to Andy as they went upstairs.

Andy got into his bed. He punched his pillow and put his head down. Then, just before he closed his eyes, he looked out his window.

It was on again! The same light was on in the Perlmans' house, in the room Tamika used to sleep in, the room just opposite Andy's.

There is *someone over there,* Andy thought. *When I made all that noise, I must have woken him up. Now, don't turn off that light, Mr. Someone . . . or whoever you are. Don't do anything. I'll be right back.*

Chapter 5
Andy and the Police

Andy hurried out of his bed again. When he was in the middle of the hall, he stopped. He ran back to his room to check if the light in the Perlmans' house was still on.

It was.

Andy banged on the door to Tamika and Rachel's room, and on the one to his parents' room.

The doors to the two bedrooms opened.

"It's on again," Andy said, really excited. "The light in the Perlmans' house is on again!"

"Stop it!" Rachel told him. "Just *stop* it! I'm tired of going to sleep and getting up and going to sleep and getting up."

Mr. Russell rubbed his eyes, yawned, and said, "Just pull your shade down and go to sleep."

"We have work tomorrow," Mrs. Russell said. "We have to sleep."

"Just come to my room and look," Andy said. "There's a light on next door, and that means there's someone inside the house."

Finally, everyone followed Andy into his room and looked out his window. The light was still on.

"OK, there's a light on," Rachel said. "Now can I please go back to sleep?"

"The Perlmans asked us to watch the house," Tamika said, "and that's just what Andy is doing."

They watched a while longer. The light remained on, but nothing else happened.

"Maybe the Perlmans set the light on a timer," Mrs. Russell said.

"They did set some lights to go on," Tamika said, "but not at this time of night and not in my room."

"Maybe it's a loose bulb," Mr. Russell suggested.

"I don't think so," Andy said. "If it was loose, it would have gone on before. And it didn't."

They all stood there a while longer. Then Andy said, "I think we should call the police."

"Maybe you're right," Mr. Russell said.

Mr. Russell called the police. He told them about the garbage and the light. "It may not be a real emergency," he said, "but it's worrisome."

They waited downstairs, in the living room. Tamika, Rachel, and Mr. and Mrs. Russell sat by the window and watched for the police.

Andy was too nervous to sit still. He ran from the living room, where he watched for the police car, to the dining room, where he looked out at the Perlmans' house to see if the light was still on. Then, just when he saw a police car turn onto his block, the light in the Perlmans' house went off.

"Great," Andy said. "*Now* it goes off!"

The car stopped in front of the Perlmans' house. Two police officers got out, each holding a flashlight. Everyone at the Russells' house watched as the police slowly approached the Perlmans' house. They waited as the police walked around the house. Then the police came next door to talk to the Russells.

"We checked the house," a tall police officer with a red moustache said. There was a tag, JOHNSON, on the front of his uniform. "Everything looks to be in order."

"But what about the light and the garbage?" Andy asked.

The other police officer said, "Maybe the homeowners put the light on a timer, or maybe there's a loose bulb." He was tall, too, and had KIRKWOOD on his tag. "And maybe one of their neighbors left some garbage. People do that, you know, to make it seem like there's someone home."

"Thank you," Mr. Russell said. "We just wanted to be sure no one had broken in."

"Wait a minute! Wait a minute!" Andy said. "There isn't a timer or a loose bulb. There can't be. I sleep opposite that room, and the light hasn't gone on until now."

"We checked the house," Officer Johnson said impatiently. "We didn't find anything unusual over there."

"Tell me, please," Andy said, "why someone would suddenly deliver garbage to the Perlmans'."

"We checked the house," Officer Johnson said

again. "There were no signs of a break-in. That's all we can do."

The two police officers returned to their car and drove off.

Rachel and Mrs. Russell went to their rooms. Andy, Tamika, and Mr. Russell went to the dining room and looked out the window at the Perlmans' house. The house was dark.

"This is all so strange," Tamika said.

"And spooky," Andy added.

They watched the Perlmans' house for a while until Mr. Russell said, "Nothing is going to happen tonight. Come on. It's time to go to sleep."

Andy and Tamika went to their rooms. Andy was sure he was too worried about what might be happening at the Perlmans' to sleep. But he wasn't. Soon after he got into bed, he was fast asleep.

Chapter 6
Stacy Ann's Great Idea

I'll eat fast, Andy told himself at breakfast the next morning. *I'll eat real fast, so before the bus comes, I'll have time to check the Perlmans' house.*

Andy spilled some cereal into his bowl. He poured on some milk and quickly ate the cereal, stuffing one spoonful after another into his mouth.

Rachel said, "There's milk and cereal dripping down your chin."

Andy looked down. He tried to see his chin, but he couldn't.

Rachel stood by the toaster oven. She had put two slices of bread in and set the timer for two minutes. Now she was waiting for the bell to ring. Then she would put American cheese on each slice of bread and put it in the toaster oven again, this time for exactly one minute.

"You shouldn't rush breakfast," Rachel told Andy. "It's the most important meal of the day."

"Did you hear that?" Andy asked his spoonful of cereal. "Rachel says you're important."

Tamika came into the kitchen for breakfast. Andy told her why he was in such a hurry. "I'll eat fast, too," Tamika said, "and I'll meet you outside."

Andy finished his cereal. He put the bowl and spoon in the sink and wiped his chin.

"Have a nice day at school," Andy's mother said to him as she walked into the kitchen. "And don't worry about the Perlmans' house. The police checked it out."

And I'll keep checking it out, Andy told himself.

Andy grabbed his backpack and lunch and hurried outside. The street wasn't so quiet now. People were on their way to work. The Belmont girls, who lived down the block, were already at the bus stop.

Detective Andy Russell is on the job again, Andy thought as he stood in front of the Perlmans' house.

The house looked the same to him. The door was closed. The lights were off. The shades downstairs were down, and the ones upstairs were up.

Andy walked slowly to the side of the house. The shades in the study were still up. Andy walked quietly to one of the windows. He got on his toes and looked in. He saw his reflection in the mirror again, but this time he wasn't frightened by it. He looked around the study. Everything looked the same.

"Hey," someone said.

"YIKES!" Andy shouted.

He dropped his books and very slowly turned. It was Tamika.

"You scared me," Andy said.

Tamika looked through the window. Then she said, "Let's hurry. Let's check the rest of the house before the bus gets here."

The lights in back were off, too, and the shades were the way they were the day before. Andy lifted the lid off the garbage can. There was still just one bag in there. The torn box of Oat Bran Toasties was still on top.

Toot! Toot!

"That's the bus," Tamika said.

Andy and Tamika ran to the front yard. They looked both ways and then quickly crossed the street. When they got to the bus, they both thanked the driver, Mr. Cole, for waiting.

"I'm used to waiting for you," Mr. Cole said. Then he asked, "And do you know how long bus drivers should wait?" Mr. Cole waited. When neither Andy nor Tamika answered, he said, "Long bus drivers should wait the same way short bus drivers wait."

Mr. Cole laughed.

"Oh," Andy said, and looked at Tamika.

Tamika smiled and rolled her eyes.

During the ride to school, Andy kept thinking about the Perlmans' house. He imagined a one-legged pirate hopping up and down the Perlmans' stairs, turning lights on and off, and laughing.

When Andy got to class, he opened his notebook, copied the homework assignment, looked up at his teacher, Ms. Roman, and waited. The first lesson was history, something about the Revolutionary War. Andy wasn't sure what Ms. Roman said. He wasn't really listening. But he *looked* like he was listening. Throughout the lesson, he stared straight at Ms. Roman. He even pretended to take notes. But he really had no idea what she was talking about. All he could think about was the Perlmans' house.

Stacy Ann Jackson, the girl who sat right in front of Andy, closed her notebook, so Andy did, too. She folded her hands and looked up at Ms. Roman, so that's what Andy did.

I'm getting good at this, Andy thought. *Ms. Roman actually thinks I'm listening.*

Some days Andy was so deep in his own dream world that he didn't hear the lunch bell ring. But this time he heard it.

In the cafeteria Andy bought a container of chocolate milk. Then he sat with Tamika and their friends Bruce Jeffries and Stacy Ann Jackson. Andy unwrapped his jelly sandwich and bit into it.

"What are you writing about?" Stacy Ann asked Andy.

"I'm not writing. I'm eating," he answered.

"Well," Stacy Ann said, "I'm writing about a

kitten in the Revolutionary War. It's going to meet everyone—George Washington, Paul Revere, Molly Pitcher, and Thomas Jefferson. It may even help write the Declaration of Independence. And I'm calling the cat Cobalt, just like *our* Cobalt."

Andy and Stacy Ann took care of a kitten that lived in the school yard. The kitten had dark gray, almost silver, fur. Andy named it Cobalt, after the silvery metal. They brought food for it.

Bruce said, "I'm going to write about a talking dog named King that thinks it's a lion, the king of the beasts. The dog will even try to roar."

What are they talking about? Andy wondered.

Tamika said, "I'm writing about a girl who can't be with her parents for a while, so she lives with different families. She'll be happy and unhappy, all at the same time."

"What are you talking about?" Andy asked.

"Weren't you listening?" Stacy Ann asked. "Ms. Roman said that tomorrow in class we'll be writing stories. She wanted us to think about what we'll write."

"Oh," Andy said. "Was that what she said?"

"You were there," Stacy Ann told Andy.

"Only his body was there," Tamika said. "His mind was somewhere else."

"It was?" Bruce said in wonderment. "You can do that? If I could, I'd have my mind at the beach, making a sand castle."

"I was thinking about the Perlmans' house," Andy said. Then he and Tamika told Stacy Ann and Bruce about the garbage, lights, and police.

"That's so strange," Stacy Ann said. She wrote on her empty lunch bag, *Mysterious garbage and a light that goes on in the middle of the night.*

"And the shade in the study," Tamika added, "which was down and now it's up."

"Hey," Andy told Stacy Ann, "that's a great idea. Make a list of clues."

"But those are the only clues we have," Tamika said.

"Oh no. We have the garbage clues." Andy told Stacy Ann and Bruce what he and Tamika had found in the garbage.

Stacy Ann wrote those on her lunch bag, too. Then she looked at the bag. "Skim milk!" she said, and gave the bag to Andy. "That tastes bad. And purple stockings, that's bad taste."

Tamika laughed and said, "Andy thinks there's a thin, one-legged man living at the Perlmans'."

"I just got a great idea," Stacy Ann said. "You could make that your story. You could write what you imagine is going on there."

Andy thought for a moment. Then he smiled and said, "Thanks, Stacy Ann. That *is* what I'll write. I imagine all sorts of weird things are happening at the Perlmans'."

Chapter 7
I'll Scare Him Out

That afternoon Andy tried to pay attention in class. Ms. Roman was explaining how plants grow. When she showed the class an illustration of the different parts of a leaf, Andy imagined that somewhere there was a classroom of young plants and a large plant was explaining to them how people grow.

"This brown bubbly stuff is called soda," Andy imagined the large plant said. *"And this brown, round disk is made from a dead animal. It's called*

a burger. This one looks almost the same, but it's a cookie. People seem to like to eat brown stuff. It all goes into people through this door with teeth. The door is called the mouth." Andy opened and closed his "door with teeth." He imagined a class of plants was watching him.

"Fractions are parts of things," Ms. Roman said.

Andy looked up. Ms. Roman was teaching math now, about halves and quarters and other fractions. Andy had trouble paying attention during that lesson, too.

Throughout the afternoon Andy kept his notebook open. He kept his eyes on Ms. Roman, but his mind was elsewhere. He thought about the Perlmans' house and what might be happening there. *This is schoolwork, too,* he told himself. *I'm thinking about the story I'll write tomorrow.*

Andy thought about the garbage. He decided someone must be living there. *Thieves don't eat breakfast in a house they rob, and they don't take out the garbage. Only someone who lives someplace does those things.* Andy thought again about the one boot he found in the garbage. *Maybe the thief doesn't have one leg. Maybe he has three,* Andy thought. *He'd have to buy two pairs of boots and have one extra. Maybe he has five legs or seven!*

The school bell rang. It was time to go home.

"I was very pleased with your work today," Ms. Roman told Andy as he was on his way out of class. "You seemed to be paying close attention to the lesson."

"Sure, Ms. Roman," Andy said.

He tried to imagine a seven-legged thief. He tried to imagine Ms. Roman with seven legs.

Andy shivered. A seven-legged Ms. Roman was just too frightening an image.

"Over here!" Bruce yelled when Andy stepped onto the bus. "I saved you a seat."

Andy walked past Rachel and Tamika to the seat Bruce had saved for him in the back of the bus.

"I didn't get all that stuff about plants," Bruce said.

"Listen," Andy told Bruce, "plants probably don't get all this stuff about us, how we do things. But right now I don't care about that. I have to worry about the Perlmans' house."

Bruce nodded.

"And right now I think there is someone living in it. And if there is, then Tamika and I have to get him out."

"How are you going to do that?"

"First I have to be sure someone is in there. *That's* what I have to do first."

Bruce turned and looked out the window of the bus. And Andy thought about how to get rid of a one-legged man, or a three- or five- or seven-legged man.

Maybe I'll scare him out. I'll bang on the windows and hide, or maybe I'll let my pet snake, Slither, in through the mail slot. Some people are afraid of snakes.

The bus stopped.

Or maybe once I can prove he's in there, I'll call the police again.

"Excuse me," Bruce said. "I have to get off."

Andy let Bruce out. Then he got ready to get off, too.

Rachel was the first one off at the next stop. Then the Belmont girls, Tamika, and Andy got off.

"Look," Rachel said. "There's a package by our door."

Andy, Tamika, and Rachel hurried across the

street. They hoped the package was the surprise from Mrs. Perlman. But it was just something for Mr. Russell.

Rachel took the package inside.

Right by the front door, inside, was a large wooden maze, with one end labeled START and the other labeled FINISH.

"Great!" Rachel said. "Now I can start on my experiment. And you promised you'd help me," she told Andy.

"Before he helps you, and before we do our homework, we're going next door," Tamika said, "to check the Perlmans' house."

Andy and Tamika left their backpacks in the hall and went outside again. The front of the Perlman house looked the same as it did in the morning. The door was closed. The lights were off. The shades downstairs were down, and the ones upstairs were up.

They went to the side of the house. The shades in Dr. Perlman's study were still up.

Andy and Tamika walked slowly toward the house. Tamika got on her toes and looked in.

"Oh, wow." Tamika gasped and quickly bent down, away from the window.

"What?" Andy asked.

"That soda can and that cup weren't on the desk yesterday," Tamika whispered.

"Are you sure?"

Tamika nodded.

"Let's get out of here," Andy whispered. "This is spooky."

"Yeah," Tamika said. She slowly backed away from the window. Then she and Andy ran next door. When they were both inside, Andy locked the door. He leaned against it. He was panting.

Chapter 8
LOOK! LOOK!

When Andy and Tamika got inside the house, Rachel was waiting for them.

"I put the maze downstairs," she said, "so we can get started with the experiment."

"Not yet," Andy told her. "Not yet."

Andy and Tamika hurried to the dining room. Rachel followed them. They all looked out the window at the Perlmans' house.

"I don't see anything," Tamika said.

"I don't, either," Andy said.

Tamika told Rachel about the cup and soda can.

"That *is* weird," Rachel said.

They watched the Perlmans' house for a while, but nothing happened.

"Come on," Rachel finally urged. "Let's go downstairs."

"Just a minute," Andy said. "A detective always writes down his clues." He took Stacy Ann's lunch bag out of his backpack. He wrote *Cup and soda can* on the bag.

Andy took one last look at the Perlmans' house. Then he followed Rachel to the basement.

Tamika stayed upstairs to watch the house.

Alongside the maze Rachel had set sticky labels, a bunch of colored markers, a chart, a stopwatch, and a camera.

"First you have to take the gerbils out of their tank and put labels on them," Rachel said. "Then I'll time them as they run through the maze."

First I *have to take the gerbils out and put labels on them!* Andy thought. He realized Rachel didn't plan to actually touch the gerbils.

"Why don't *you* take the gerbils out," Andy said, "and *I'll* time them."

"Because they're *your* gerbils and this is *my* watch."

"Oh," Andy said. "Well, first I have to make sure all my pets have food, that they're all OK. Then I'll help you."

"Hi, Sylvia," Andy said to the goldfish as he sprinkled some flakes of food into its tank. "How was your day?"

He watched the goldfish swim to the top of the tank and eat.

"And how are you?" he asked Slither, his garter snake.

Slither stuck out his forked tongue.

Next Andy looked in the gerbil tank. He watched the gerbils run through the plastic tunnels and on the treadmill. He fed them. Then he said, "I need a volunteer. Which one of you wants to take an IQ test?"

Rachel was impatient. "This is ridiculous," she said. "Do you expect one to raise its tail and shout, 'Pick me!'?"

"You're the one who's testing them," Andy said. "Like it really matters if one is smarter than the others! All that really matters is that they're happy!"

"They're happy," Rachel assured Andy. "Now could we please get going?"

Andy looked into one of the tanks. He took out one of the gerbils and held it near Rachel. "Meet your psychologist," Andy told the gerbil.

"Very funny," Rachel said.

Andy gently put a label, which Rachel had colored red, onto the gerbil's tail. He put the gerbil in the maze, at the end marked START.

"Go!" Rachel called, and pressed the button on the top of the stopwatch.

The gerbil didn't go. It looked around. It sniffed the wood. But it didn't try to find its way through the maze.

"Go on!" Rachel urged. "Go on!" But the gerbil didn't go on. It continued to look and sniff.

"See? This proves Red is a smart gerbil," Andy said. "It's thinking, *Why should I run through this maze? What's in it for me?*"

Red took a few steps forward and stopped again to look and sniff.

Andy told Rachel, "You have to give the gerbil a reason to go through the maze."

"Don't you want to do well?" Rachel asked the gerbil. "Don't you want everyone in school to know you're the smartest one?"

Andy looked at Rachel. "I hope you're joking," he said. "Wait here," Andy told his sister. "I'll give Red a real reason to go through the maze."

Andy ran upstairs. He got a box of raisins from the pantry and some cheese from the refrigerator. Then, before he went downstairs again, he asked Tamika if she had seen anything unusual at the Perlmans' house. She hadn't. Andy looked out the dining room window. The shades next door seemed the same to him. He didn't see lights on or anyone outside the house.

Andy told Tamika, "Let me know if you see anything." Then he hurried downstairs.

Andy took Red out of the maze. He put some raisins and cheese at the end of the maze marked FINISH. Then he put the gerbil at START again, and Rachel pressed the button on the top of her stopwatch.

Red sniffed. It smelled the raisins and cheese and tried to find its way through the maze. It bumped into the walls of the maze lots of times and made a few wrong turns. Then, at last, it found its way to FINISH.

Rachel pressed the button on her stopwatch and announced, "One minute, forty-three seconds." She wrote that on her chart and said, "Let's get another one."

"Oh no," Andy said. "Not yet. Red went all the way through this maze to get a treat. Now let him eat."

They watched Red eat some raisins and cheese. When Red was done, Rachel took its picture. Then Andy returned it to the tank.

Andy took another gerbil from the tank. He put a blue-marked label on the gerbil's tail. Then Andy spoke to his pet. "Now, Blue, I am going to put you in a maze. You just do the best you can getting through it. No matter how long it takes you, the raisins and cheese will be waiting for you."

Andy put the gerbil in at START, and Rachel timed it as it made its way through the maze.

Andy and Rachel tested five gerbils, Red, Blue, Purple, Green, and Gray. The gerbil with the green label made it through the fastest. Andy congratulated Green. Then Rachel took a few pictures of the winner.

Andy thanked the gerbils for their help. "Now you thank them, too," he told his sister.

Rachel leaned over the gerbil tank and said, "Thank you," but Andy could tell she didn't mean it.

When his parents came home, Andy told them about the cup and soda can. They both thought it was strange. But they weren't ready to call the police again until they were sure someone had broken into the house.

"Maybe yesterday you just didn't notice it," Mrs. Russell said.

But Andy and Tamika *knew* the can and cup hadn't been there the day before. And they were determined to find out how they had got there.

Andy and Tamika did their homework by Andy's window. They looked out often at the Perlmans' house, but nothing happened. That night Andy planned to wait up and watch for a light to be turned on next door. But he hadn't had much sleep the night before. He was tired, and soon after he got into bed, he was asleep.

The next morning, after breakfast, Andy and Tamika checked the Perlmans' house again. The front door was closed. The shades were down.

Tamika told Andy, "We should really go to the side of the house and look into Jonathan's study."

"Yeah," Andy said. "We should."

Andy looked at Tamika. Neither moved. Neither wanted to look in the study window.

Then they saw the bus coming. They were happy to see it. Now they *couldn't* look through the window. They quickly crossed the street.

"Why do you keep snooping around?" the tall Belmont girl asked them. "You know that's trespassing, don't you? It's against the law."

"We're watching, not snooping," Andy told her. "Mrs. Perlman asked us to."

The bus stopped and the door opened. Tamika and Rachel got on and sat together, near the front of the bus. Andy sat near the back, next to Bruce. Mr. Cole pulled the lever, closed the bus door, and drove off. The bus turned the corner, and Andy looked out the window as they passed the Russells' and Perlmans' houses.

"LOOK! LOOK!" Andy called out. "Did you see that?"

The front door of the Perlmans' house was open.

Andy ran to the front of the bus.

"You have to stop," he told Mr. Cole.

"Are you sick?" Mr. Cole asked.

"No."

"Then I don't have to stop. But you have to sit down."

"But the door to the Perlmans' house was open. There's a thief!"

"When you get to school, you can tell your teacher or tell the principal, but right now you have to get in your seat!"

"Did you see it?" Andy asked Tamika and Rachel as he walked past them to the back of the bus.

Neither Tamika nor Rachel had seen the open door.

"Are you sure the door was open?" Tamika asked.

"Sure I'm sure," Andy answered.

"*You* saw it, didn't you?" Andy asked Bruce when he sat down again.

Bruce shook his head.

"Why didn't you? You were sitting right here! Don't you ever look out the window?"

"I'm sorry," Bruce said.

When Andy and Tamika got to school, they went straight to the office.

"I have to call my parents," Andy told Mrs. Clark, the principal's secretary.

She let him use the telephone on her desk. He dialed his home and waited. No one answered.

The school bell rang. He had to get to class. *Now what do I do?* he wondered.

Tamika told Mrs. Clark what had happened.

"It all sounds very odd," Mrs. Clark said. "Are you sure the door was open?"

"Everyone keeps asking me that," Andy said. "Of course I'm sure."

"This is not a school matter," Mrs. Clark said. "This is something for the police."

She looked at a paper with emergency numbers she had on her desk. Then she picked up the telephone receiver and dialed the police.

Chapter 9
Trapped in School

Mrs. Clark told the police officer about Andy, Tamika, the Perlmans' trip to South America, and the open front door. Then she gave the telephone to Andy. "He wants to talk to you," she said.

"Where are you?" the police officer asked.

"I'm at school," he said quickly. He told the officer the Perlmans' address and said, "Please tell Officers Johnson and Kirkwood about the open door. They'll know what I'm talking about."

"I'll tell them," the officer said. "Now, don't worry. Just go to class. We'll take care of everything."

Andy put the telephone receiver down. "That's the problem. We'll be in class while who knows what might be happening at the Perlmans'."

Andy and Tamika thanked Mrs. Clark and hurried to class.

"You're late," Ms. Roman told them when they entered the room. "Get to your seats. We have work to do."

There was a DO NOW on the board, a list of science words for Andy and his classmates to copy into their notebooks: *chloroplast, glucose, starch, carbon dioxide, photosynthesis,* and *cell respiration.*

Andy copied the words into his science notebook.

There was a potted plant with large leaves on Ms. Roman's desk. Ms. Roman turned over one of the leaves. Andy smiled, folded his hands, and put them on his desk. He looked right at Ms. Roman and the plant.

Who opened the Perlmans' door? Andy wondered. He hadn't seen a car or truck in front of the Perlmans' house. *Maybe the thief parked his car in the garage,* Andy thought. *He was just leaving this morning and saw me waiting at the bus stop, so he quickly ran inside.*

"Andy!" Ms. Roman said loudly. "Do plants make food?"

" 'Do plants make food?' " Andy repeated, and looked around. It seemed everyone in class was looking at him.

He tried to imagine a plant making a pizza. It seemed so ridiculous. He was about to say no, but he saw Stacy Ann Jackson in the seat just in front of his nod and whisper, "Yes."

"Yes," Andy told Ms. Roman. "Plants make food."

"What kind of food do they make?"

Pizza, Andy thought, but he didn't say it.

Andy looked at the plant on Ms. Roman's desk and at its large green leaves. *Lettuce is a plant,* Andy thought, *and parsley is, too, and peppers and tomatoes grow on plants.*

"Plants make salads," Andy said.

"People make salads," Ms. Roman told Andy. "Plants make glucose. It's a form of sugar."

"Oh," Andy said.

"Plants use energy from sunlight to combine

carbon dioxide from the air and water to make glucose. This process is called *photosynthesis.*"

"Oh," Andy said again.

"The carbon dioxide gets into the plant through very small holes in the backs of leaves. The water gets into the plant through the roots."

Why do I have to know this stuff? Andy wondered. *Plants don't know how I make popcorn, so why should I know how plants make glucose?*

Andy tried to pay attention during the rest of the lesson. Ms. Roman spoke about chloroplasts and chlorophyll and showed the class a picture of what the back of a leaf looks like through a microscope.

Andy thought it was a waste of time to be talking about all that chloro stuff while the Perlmans' house was being robbed. But he didn't want to get into trouble. He just couldn't allow himself to be kept after school—not today.

Ms. Roman taught math next, how to add fractions. Andy did his best to pay attention, but it was a real struggle. He was glad when the bell rang for lunch.

Lunch! Andy thought, and he remembered the clues he had listed on Stacy Ann's lunch bag. He took it out of his pocket and added *Open door* to the list.

"Remember," Ms. Roman told the class, "when you get back from lunch, you'll be writing stories."

In the cafeteria Andy stood by the lunch table and told Stacy Ann and Bruce, as dramatically as he could, "This morning, while we've been in school, the police have probably been real busy. I bet they arrested a killer crook who was robbing the Perlmans. There may even be a reward."

"I can't stand not knowing what's happening," Tamika said.

"Cream cheese again," Bruce complained. "I get so little for lunch, and it's the same stuff every day."

"Is food all you think about?" Andy asked Bruce, and gave him a cupcake. Tamika gave Bruce half of her tuna fish sandwich. Stacy Ann gave him a plum.

"I need to know what's happening at the Perlmans'," Andy said. "I'm calling the police."

"Wait," Bruce said. He pushed most of Andy's cupcake into his mouth. Then he took a big bite of Tamika's tuna fish sandwich and a sip of juice. His mouth was stuffed. Juice was dripping down his chin. Bruce was about to bite into his cream cheese sandwich when Tamika grabbed his hand.

"Swallow," she told him.

Bruce swallowed.

"I might be a hero," Andy said. "After all, I'm the one who saw the open door this morning. And I'm the one who spoke to the police." Then he turned to Tamika and told her, "But if there's a reward, we're sharing it. We're both watching the house, so we share the reward."

"Thank you," Tamika said.

"The office phone is just for emergencies," Andy told his friends when they were in the hall, "and this isn't an emergency anymore, so I'll have to call the police station. I'll call from the hall phone."

Andy looked through the telephone book hanging by the public phone. He found the number for the police station. He put a few coins into the slot, entered the number, and waited.

A woman answered.

"Hello," Andy said into the receiver. "Is Officer Johnson or Officer Kirkwood there? This is Andy Russell."

"Just a minute."

Andy waited.

"Kirkwood here. Can I help you?"

"Yes. This is Andy Russell. I'm the boy who called this morning about the open door at the Perlman house. Did you catch him? Did you catch the thief?"

"No," Officer Kirkwood said. He sounded annoyed. "We didn't catch anyone. All we did was waste some time. The doors were all closed. The windows were all shut."

"Oh," Andy said.

"We'll keep an eye on the house. Someone will drive past there at least once a day, but we don't think there's anything to worry about."

"Oh. Thank you," Andy said.

Officer Kirkwood hung up.

Andy slowly put the telephone down and turned to face his friends.

Chapter 10
I'm a Criminal

What did he say?" Tamika asked.

"Are you a hero?" Bruce wanted to know. "Are you getting a reward?"

"No," Andy answered softly. He was embarrassed. "I'm not a hero. I'm a pest."

Rrrr!

The bell rang. Lunch period was over.

"A pest," Bruce said, and thought for a moment. "That's not good."

"I bet right now," Andy said, "next to all the

police WANTED posters is a picture of me on a NOT WANTED poster." He stopped by the door to their classroom. "I tried to be a hero, and I feel like a criminal. The police hate me."

"No one hates you," Tamika said.

"Are you coming in or not?" Ms. Roman called out. She had her hands on her hips and an impatient look on her face.

"What did you say about no one hating me?" Andy mumbled as he walked into class.

Ms. Roman had written *DON'T THINK! JUST WRITE!* in large letters across the board. There were two sheets of paper on each desk.

When everyone was seated, Ms. Roman told the class, "Use your imaginations. Have fun with your stories. Remember, what you're writing is just a first draft."

Andy looked at the two blank sheets of paper.

I'm a criminal, he wrote, *wanted by the police. I didn't do anything wrong, but that doesn't matter. They have my picture posted everywhere, in candy stores and on trees under the LOST KITTEN signs. I can't go to school and I can't go home.*

Andy looked at what he had written. It filled just

the top of one sheet of paper. He had to write more.

I hide, he wrote. *I hide in toolsheds and garages. Hey,* Andy thought, *I know where I'd hide.*

I hide, he wrote, *in the houses of people who are on vacation or are away in places like South America. But I can never rest. Children and neighbors are my enemies. They peek in my windows and in my garbage cans.*

Andy had almost filled the entire first sheet of paper. He poked Stacy Ann. "How much have you written?" he asked.

She showed him that both sheets of her paper were covered with her neat handwriting. She raised her hand and asked Ms. Roman for more paper.

But I do have fun, Andy wrote. *I spook children. I turn lights on and I turn them off. But I can't buy food in candy stores or supermarkets. The police would catch me there. I have to go to health food stores and buy yucky stuff like oats and green tea.*

"Finish up," Ms. Roman said. "The bell will ring in a few minutes."

How do I end this? Andy wondered. *I know! Why are the police after me? Why am I a wanted criminal?* he wrote. *I'm wanted because I went to a public bathroom. The sign by the paper towels said* TAKE ONE, *but I took two! And that's why I'm a criminal—wanted by the police.*

Rrrr!

"Leave your papers on your desks," Ms. Roman told the class. "I look forward to reading them."

Chapter 11
ROAR!

ndy took a last look at his paper. " 'I'm a Criminal—Wanted by the Police,' " Andy read. *There must be some reason I shouldn't have written this,* Andy thought. *I bet this story gets me in trouble.*

"Hurry," Bruce called to him, "or we'll miss the bus."

Andy grabbed his story. He was about to put it in his backpack when Ms. Roman told him, "You don't have to bring it to me. Just leave your story on your desk. I'll collect it."

Andy put the story back. He took his backpack and hurried out of the classroom, out of the school, and onto the bus. Bruce had saved him a seat again, right behind Tamika and Rachel.

"Do you know what I wrote?" Bruce asked. "I wrote about a boy named Bryce who has a dog named King, and the dog thinks he's really a lion, the king of the jungle. Isn't that great? The dog roars like this: ROAR! ROAR!"

Tamika and Rachel turned.

"ROAR!"

Bruce explained, "I'm telling Andy about my story."

"And I have something to tell Andy," Rachel said. "I have some really good news."

"The dog's name is King, and it ROARS like a lion and scares the postman."

"My science teacher really loved the experiment," Rachel said. "She wants me to demonstrate it to the class."

"That's great," Tamika said.

Bruce went on with his story. "And the postman

thinks there's really a lion in the house. And Bryce's father is real angry because the postman doesn't leave the mail, and he wants the mail."

"So I need you to let me use your gerbils again," Rachel said. "And I need you to come to my class and show everyone what we did. So will you do that?"

"Hey," Bruce said. "Are you listening to my story about King? Are you, Andy?"

"Yes, yes," Andy answered Bruce.

"Great," Rachel said. "Thank you. Thank you. We'll bring the maze and gerbils in tomorrow."

"What's great?" Andy asked.

"Hey, this is my stop," Bruce said, and grabbed his backpack. "Let me get out."

Bruce had grabbed his backpack upside down. As he squeezed past Andy, his books, papers, and an apple fell out. There were a few open windows, and papers flew all over the bus. Bruce grabbed his science and math books. He reached under the seat and got his notebook.

"Let's go! Let's go!" Mr. Cole called out.

Bruce grabbed the apple and some papers. He shoved them into his backpack and hurried off the bus.

"Wait! Wait!" a small girl near the front of the bus called. She waved a paper and said, "You forgot this."

"And this, too," someone else called out.

But Bruce was off the bus, and the bus was already moving.

"I'll take them," Andy said. He grabbed his own backpack and went to the front of the bus.

"Tell your friend to study more," the girl said as she gave the paper to Andy.

It was a test paper. *I shouldn't look at it,* Andy thought, but as he put it into his backpack, he just couldn't help looking. *Sixty-one on a science test! She's right. Bruce should study more.*

Andy collected the other papers. The bus stopped and Andy got off. He looked across the street at the Perlmans' house. The door was closed. The shades were the same as they had been in the morning.

The Belmont girls, Tamika, and Rachel got off the bus.

"We should practice with the gerbils, so they'll know what to do tomorrow," Rachel said. "I don't want them to embarrass me in front of my whole class."

"What are you talking about?" Andy asked.

Tamika told him.

"When did I say I would go to your class?" Andy asked Rachel. "I have enough trouble with Ms. Roman in fourth grade, so why would I want to go to sixth grade with you?"

"When you're helping Rachel in her class," Tamika told Andy, "you won't have to be in Ms. Roman's class."

When Andy heard that, he agreed to help Rachel.

Rachel unlocked the door to the Russells' house. Tamika and Rachel went to the kitchen, where they had snacks. Andy went to the basement. First he fed his pets. Then he looked for the five gerbils with labels stuck to their tails.

Three gerbils, Red, Blue, and Purple, still had their labels on. Andy found the green and gray labels on the floor of the tank. Andy reached in for the labels and asked, "Which one of you wants to be Green? Which one of you wants to be Gray?"

None of the gerbils volunteered.

"Come on," Andy urged. "Green got the best score."

Andy waited. When he still had no volunteers, he reached into the tank and picked one and put the green label on it. He put the gray label on another gerbil.

"You'll like this," he told them. "You'll get to travel on the bus, where you'll meet Mr. Cole, the driver. He's nice. You'll go to school and meet lots of kids. Some of them are nice, too. And you'll get to eat raisins and cheese."

Andy put the screen back on the top of the tank.

"Are there any questions?" Andy asked the gerbils. There weren't any, so he went upstairs to do his homework.

Andy and Tamika did their homework in Andy's room again, by his window. Andy looked out the window often, at the Perlmans' house. But nothing happened.

Andy did his homework quickly.

"That's it," he announced, and closed his books. "I'm done."

Andy watched Tamika do her work. He watched her look through the geography book very carefully before she answered any of the questions at the end of the chapter.

"This isn't a test," Andy told her. "It's just home-work."

Tamika ignored him. She continued to do her work. While she worked, Andy thought about the Perlmans' house and about Rachel's gerbil experiment. He decided to watch the Perlmans' house from his window and if he saw something suspicious, he would tell his father. Let *him* call the police. And he decided that if Rachel was doing experiments with gerbils, *she* would have to touch and hold them.

When Tamika finished her work, Andy told her about all his decisions.

"You're right about the police, but I don't think you'll get Rachel to hold the gerbils."

Andy was *sure* he would.

Chapter 12
There's Someone in There

Andy went into Rachel's room and told her, "There's a lot to do to get ready for tomorrow. We've got to pack up the raisins and cheese. I've got to get Dad's old toolbox ready to take the gerbils to school. And you've got to practice handling the gerbils."

"I've got to what?"

"You don't want your teacher and all your friends to see that you're afraid of a few tiny animals, do you? Your teacher may even think that you didn't do the experiment, that I did everything."

Rachel looked at her hands.

"Let's go," Andy said. "It will be fun."

"It will be fun for you," Rachel said as she got up, "but not for me."

It sure will be fun, Andy thought as Tamika and Rachel followed him into the basement.

When they were by the tank with the labeled gerbils, Andy told Rachel, "It's important to talk to them, so they get to know your voice."

Rachel looked at Tamika, who nodded and told her Andy was right.

"But what do I say to them?" Rachel asked.

"Introduce yourself," Tamika said. "Tell them about yourself. Tell them about school."

Rachel leaned over the top of the tank. "Hello. I'm Rachel Russell," she said. "I'm in the sixth grade, and I'm interested in literature and history."

Rachel turned to Andy and Tamika and said, "I feel silly and, anyway, I don't think they're listening."

"They hear the sound of your voice," Andy told her. "After they get used to it, you can practice holding them."

"I'd rather talk to them."

Rachel told the gerbils about her favorite author, Mark Twain, and about his books. She told them she hoped to go to college and become a high school English teacher. She told the gerbils about her teachers and her homework and about how her mom was pregnant.

"I think they've heard enough," Andy said. "I know *I* have."

Andy reached into the tank and took out Gray. "To a gerbil," Andy said, "your hands are very big, so you must move them slowly. Don't scare Gray."

Tamika showed Rachel how to hold her hands.

"It's a long drop to the floor, so you have to hold Gray against your body," Andy said, "so if it gets scared and jumps, it will land on you and not on the floor."

"Land on me! I'm not doing this."

"You're a puzzle to me, a real jigsaw," Andy told his sister. "When the doctor holds up a big needle and points it at your arm, you don't flinch. The doctor says it won't hurt, and you know it will. And now you're scared of a tiny gerbil? Look at Gray."

Rachel looked at the gerbil moving around in Andy's hands.

"Look how small a gerbil is. To Gray you're King Kong," Andy said. Then he corrected himself. "No, you're *Queen* Kong."

Andy moved his cupped hands toward Rachel's cupped hands. Rachel clenched her teeth, closed her eyes, and waited.

"You can do this," Tamika told Rachel.

Gray looked up at Andy. Then it looked at Rachel. Gray twitched its nose and ran into Rachel's hands.

"It tickles," Rachel said.

Rachel opened her eyes and looked at Gray. She watched it run from her hands to Andy's and then back again into hers.

"What if it has to—you know?" Rachel asked.

"If it has to 'you know,' it *you knows*. Doesn't everyone?"

"Take it back," Rachel said. "NOW!"

Andy took Gray back. He returned the gerbil to its tank and took out Purple. He held it gently and taught Rachel how to pet a gerbil.

Ding! Ding!

"That's the door," Rachel said. "I have to go answer it."

"Saved by the ding-ding," Andy said, "saved by the bell."

Rachel ran up the basement stairs. Andy put Purple back in the tank. Tamika put the screen on top. Then they went upstairs, too. Rachel was by the open front door. She was holding a box wrapped in brown paper.

"It's for you," Rachel told Tamika. "It's from Ecuador."

Tamika took the package from Rachel. It was almost completely covered with tape.

"It's from the Perlmans," Tamika said. "It must be the surprise. I wonder what it is."

The delivery truck was still outside. Then Andy saw the driver, returning to the truck from next door. He had delivered a package to the Perlmans.

Tamika tried to tear the package open but couldn't. "I'll need scissors to open this," she said.

"I wonder who would send something to the Perlmans," Andy said. "They won't be home for months." He watched the delivery truck drive off.

"We can't leave a package by their front door. We have to go over there."

Reluctantly Tamika put the package on the small table by the front door. She and Rachel followed Andy outside. They went to the Perlmans'. There was no package at the Perlmans' house.

"Maybe the man rang the bell," Tamika said, "and when no one answered, he took it back into his truck."

"No," Rachel told her. "If he did that, there would be a note. And there is no note."

"There's someone in there," Andy whispered. "I hear him moving."

Bang!

There was a loud noise from inside the house.

Andy, Tamika, and Rachel jumped away from the door. They raced across the driveway to their own front lawn.

"It sounded to me like something dropped," Tamika said.

"Maybe something dropped," Andy said, "or maybe that was a gunshot!"

They waited, watched, and listened. When nothing seemed to be happening at the Perlmans' house, Tamika whispered, "What do we do now?"

"We can go over there and knock on the door," Rachel said, "or we can call the police."

Tamika looked next door. Then she looked at Andy and said, "No. I'm afraid to knock on the door. I'm afraid someone might answer it."

"And we can't call the police again," Andy said. "I know *I* can't!"

He thought for a moment. Then he said, "I know what we can do. I know just what we can do—and we should have done it a long time ago."

Chapter 13
Elke Bell

Andy hurried into his house. Tamika and Rachel followed him. He went to the kitchen and picked up the telephone.

"What are you doing?" Tamika asked.

Andy pressed the buttons on the phone.

"I thought you couldn't call the police again," Rachel said.

"Hello," a woman on the other end of the line said.

Andy held his hand to his mouth. He was too afraid to talk.

"Who is this? Who are you? You called me, remember? And if you don't have anything to say, then you shouldn't have called me. Good-bye and have a nice day."

"There's someone there," Andy told Tamika and Rachel. "There's someone in the Perlmans' house! It's a woman."

Andy told Rachel, "Make sure our front door is locked." Then he told Tamika, "Look out the window. Let me know if anyone is coming over here."

When Rachel had checked the door and Tamika was by the window, Andy pressed the telephone buttons again. The same woman answered.

"Hello."

"Hello. This is Andy Russell. I live next door, and the Perlmans asked us to watch their house. Now, I want to know what you're doing in there."

"The telephone keeps ringing and I keep answering it. That's what I'm doing. And right now I'm talking to you."

"Who is that? Who are you talking to?" Tamika asked. She left the window.

Andy gave Tamika the telephone. "I need to know who you are," Tamika said, "and what you're doing in the Perlmans' house."

"I'm Lisa Karen Bell, but people call me L. K. Those are my initials, but it's also a name, Elke, so you can call me that—Elke Bell, that's me."

"OK, so that's you," Tamika said. "But what are you doing in the Perlmans' house?"

"I'm an artist and I met Miriam in Ecuador. She said she wrote to you. She said you would be happy to meet someone she met on her trip."

"She said she had a surprise for us. I thought it would be a souvenir."

"Well, I'm not a souvenir—I'm an artist, and I know I should have come over to introduce myself. Miriam told me to, but I was so busy with my artwork and things."

Tamika put her hand over the receiver. "It's Miriam's friend," she whispered to Andy and Rachel. "She's an artist."

"Hey, do you like gumdrops?" Elke Bell asked. "I bought a big box and ate all the orange ones. Those are the best. If you want the other flavors, you can have them all."

"She doesn't stop talking," Tamika whispered, and handed the telephone back to Andy.

"When we saw the lights go on next door, we were really scared," Andy said, but Elke Bell didn't seem to hear what he was saying. She just kept talking.

Andy gave the telephone to Rachel.

"You know what?" Elke Bell said. "You should come over and see the great images and forms I've made. You really should."

The front door opened. Mr. and Mrs. Russell were home.

Andy told them about Elke Bell.

"Well, I'm glad it's not a thief," Mrs. Russell said.

Andy and Tamika helped Mr. and Mrs. Russell carry in the groceries. Rachel put the telephone receiver on the kitchen counter and went to help, too.

There were several more bags in the car. Mr. and Mrs. Russell waited by the front door as the children brought them in. Then they all carried the groceries to the kitchen.

"You forgot to hang up the telephone," Mr.

Russell said, and handed it to Andy. Elke Bell was still talking. "It's an inverted vase," she said, "with flowers on the outside."

Then Andy interrupted her. "Do you know, because of you, I called the police?"

"You did?" Elke Bell asked.

"They think I'm a big pest," Andy said.

"Am I in trouble?" Elke Bell asked. "Did I do something wrong? Some of my art is *out there*! Do you know what I mean? It's different. But that's not a crime, is it?"

"No. You're not in trouble. But I might be. I told the police the Perlmans were away and that I thought someone broke into the house. They said they would keep an eye on it. Now I have to tell them about you."

Andy gave the telephone to his mother. He got the telephone book and looked up the police precinct number.

Elke Bell told Mrs. Russell, "A lot of people love my work. It's moody stuff, expressive."

"Does she ever stop talking?" Mrs. Russell whispered to Andy. She listened for a while and then told Elke Bell, "I have to say good-bye now. We need to make another call."

100

Mrs. Russell waited and listened, but Elke didn't stop talking.

"Good-bye," Mrs. Russell said again, and hung up the telephone.

Then Mr. Russell called the police and told them about Elke Bell. He listened for a moment and then thanked the police officer.

"Was he mad?" Andy asked.

"No. He said you did the right thing when you called him. He said he wishes everyone who saw something suspicious going on would call."

"He said that?"

Mr. Russell nodded.

"But we just did the *wrong* thing with Miriam Perlman's friend," Mrs. Russell said. "Elke Bell is all alone. We should invite her over for dinner."

Mrs. Russell tried to call her, but the Perlmans' telephone line was busy. "Let's go over there," she said. "We'll knock on her door and invite her."

Andy, Tamika, and Rachel followed Mr. and Mrs. Russell outside. They all went to the Perlmans' house, and Mr. Russell knocked on the door.

They waited. A woman wearing a paint-splattered, bright orange jumpsuit opened the door. She was holding a portable telephone.

"Hello," Mrs. Russell said. "We live next door, and we'd like to invite you to have dinner with us tonight."

Elke Bell looked at the telephone she was holding. Then she looked at all the Russells and Tamika.

"Aren't I talking to you on the telephone?" she asked. "Hello," Elke Bell said into the telephone receiver. "Hello."

No one responded.

"This is all very strange," Elke Bell said. She pressed a button on the telephone and put it in the front pocket of her jumpsuit.

Andy looked at the woman standing in front of him in the orange paint-splattered jumpsuit. He listened to her talk and talk, and he thought, *You're the one who's strange.* But he didn't say it.

"We live next door," Mrs. Russell said again, "and we would like you to have dinner with us."

"And I know what you like to eat," Andy said. "You like Oat Bran Toasties."

"Yes! Yes! I love those little squares of oat."

Mrs. Russell smiled. "We don't have Toasties,"

she said, "but hopefully we'll have something you like."

"Now, if you'll please excuse us," Mr. Russell said, "we have to unpack the groceries. And we have to make dinner."

"But I want to show you my work, the images and forms I've been creating."

"Why don't you show the children?" Mr. Russell suggested. "And we'll come by after dinner."

"Wait! Wait!" Elke Bell said as Mr. and Mrs. Russell started to leave. "My gallery just sent me a whole package of brochures with pictures of my work. Here, take one."

There was a large package next to the front door. Elke Bell took a brochure from it and gave it to Mrs. Russell.

"Thank you," Mrs. Russell said. She looked at the pictures in the brochure and said, "Your work looks very . . . *interesting*."

Andy's parents left. Then Elke Bell led the children downstairs, to the Perlmans' cellar. The floor of one corner of the cellar was covered with paint-splattered sheets. There was a large floodlight set in the middle of the sheets.

"Daytime!" Elke Bell called out, and turned on the light.

Andy, Tamika, and Rachel shielded their eyes from the bright light.

There were just three small windows in the cellar, all on the wall on the side of the house not facing the Russells' house. *That's why we didn't see all this light,* Andy thought.

There was a large white box in the corner of the cellar. Set on top of it was an orange boot. A purple stocking was draped over the toe of the boot.

Mom said her stuff is interesting, Andy thought. *To me, it looks weird.*

"Follow me," Elke Bell told the children, "and lose yourselves in art."

Andy, Tamika, and Rachel stepped onto the sheets and approached the paintings. Some of the paint on the sheets was still wet. Andy looked down. There was orange paint on his sneakers.

Elke Bell pointed to the boot and said, "This is my ode to the foot, to the appendage that moves us all." She held up a collage and told the children, "And these are the forms, the shapes of life. They merge and swim together in one ocean. Dive in!"

Elke Bell talked on and on about her art, what

it all meant to her. Then she asked Andy, Tamika, and Rachel what they thought.

Tamika and Rachel both said they liked it. Andy said he liked the colors she'd used. "I don't really understand everything you told us about your art," Andy added, "but I'm only in the fourth grade. I don't have to understand everything."

Elke Bell started to explain her art all over again when her jumpsuit rang.

RING!

"Oh my," Elke Bell said. "That tickles."

RING!

"Oh my," Elke Bell said again. She laughed as she took the telephone out of the front pocket of her jumpsuit.

RING!

"Hello. It's me. Elke Bell. Thank you for calling." She listened for a moment. "That's so nice," she said. "We'll be right over."

Elke Bell pressed a button on the telephone and returned it to the pocket of her jumpsuit.

"That was your father," she said. "It's time to eat."

When they left the house, Elke Bell locked the front door. "I have to be very careful here," she whispered to the children. "I hear strange noises at night. There may be a prowler."

No, that's me, Andy thought.

Before dinner Andy threw out his lunch-bag list of clues.

This case is solved, he told himself. *Detective Andy Russell does it again!*

At dinner Elke Bell raised her hands, wiggled her fingers, and told the Russells and Tamika, "New places give me new energy. That's why I travel, why I go from one place to the next, with just my backpack and a few boxes of art supplies. I paint and sculpt until the energy is gone. Then I send the images I've created to the gallery that sells my work."

Andy watched and listened as Elke Bell moved her hands, wiggled her fingers, and talked and talked. Andy wondered what sort of energy she was getting from the dining room. He wiggled his fingers under the table to see if that would give *him* some of the room's energy. It didn't. It just made his fingers tired.

"Every few months I send the gallery large packages of art."

"Packages?" Andy said. "Mrs. Perlman sent us a package, and we haven't opened it."

Andy excused himself and hurried to the front entryway. He took the package off the table and brought it to the dining room. "It's addressed to you," he said, and gave it to Tamika.

Tamika tried again to open it but couldn't. Mr. Russell took it and pulled at the tape. The package popped open and several carved wooden animals fell out.

"A bear," Andy said as he picked up one of the animals.

"There's a lion, tiger, giraffe, monkey, walrus, elephant, rhinoceros, hippopotamus, and bison," Tamika said as she set them all around her dinner plate.

Elke Bell took the lion and studied it. "This is handmade," she said, "and very well sculpted. It's a work of art." She looked carefully at the others and said, "It's obvious Miriam admires form. I'll leave her my *Ode to the Foot* as a gift to thank her for letting me stay in her house."

Andy wondered where the Perlmans would put Elke Bell's orange boot.

"Two of the animals are for you," Tamika told Andy.

He studied them all and chose the giraffe and the walrus.

It was time for dessert and Elke Bell asked for a cup of tea. "I like green tea," she told Mrs. Russell. "It's good for me."

"We don't have green tea," Mrs. Russell said, "but we have pistachio ice cream. That's green."

"Green tea, green ice cream—whatever," Elke Bell said, and she ate two scoops of pistachio ice cream.

Andy had two scoops, too. He wasn't sure green ice cream was good for him, but he knew it tasted good.

Chapter 14
A Really Good Day

The next morning Rachel packed a bag of raisins and cheese. Andy put wood chips in the bottom of his father's old metal toolbox. Then he put Blue and Red in. (Rachel's teacher only wanted her to use two gerbils to demonstrate the experiment.) There were small holes in the sides of the box, so the gerbils could breathe. Andy carried the toolbox and Rachel took the maze, and they went outside.

When Andy got on the bus, he sat next to

Bruce. Andy gave him the papers that had fallen out of his backpack the day before. "I shouldn't have looked at them," he said, "but I did. I didn't do so well, either. Let's study together for the next science test, OK?"

"OK," Bruce said.

Then Andy told him about Elke Bell.

"She sounds like fun," Bruce said.

"She is," Andy told him.

When they got to school, Andy and Tamika went first to their class. They told Ms. Roman about Rachel's experiment and asked if they could go to Rachel's class to help out.

"Yes, you may, but hurry back. There's something special I plan to do today, but I'll wait for both of you—especially for Andy."

"Something special? You'll wait for me?"

Ms. Roman smiled.

Andy and Tamika walked past the elementary school's office to the middle school side of the building. The walls there were lined with lockers, and the halls were crowded with middle school students. Andy felt very small among all those older, much bigger children. A very tall, very strong-looking boy walked past.

"I better start growing," Andy whispered to Tamika.

Ms. Jackson, Rachel's science teacher, was in the hall, by the door to Rachel's classroom. Andy and Tamika introduced themselves to her.

"Welcome. I've heard such nice things about both of you," Ms. Jackson said. "I'm happy to meet you."

"About me?" Andy asked.

Ms. Jackson smiled.

Andy looked in the room. He saw Rachel. *I wonder what she told Ms. Jackson.* And he wondered what Rachel had told her classmates.

"Hey, Andy! Hey, Tamika!" Rachel said as she put the maze on the teacher's desk. Then she said *really* loud, "Everyone, I'd like you to meet my brother, Andy, and our friend Tamika."

Lots of Rachel's classmates shouted their greetings.

"So, you're the famous Andy Russell," one boy said. "How are you? How are Sylvia and Slither? How are your gerbils? And how is fourth grade?"

"I'm good. They're good. And it's good. How come you know so much about me?"

"Rachel talks about you all the time. She says you're funny."

"Rachel said *that*?" Andy turned to his sister and asked, "How come you said nice stuff about me?"

"Because you're my brother."

"Then how come you fight with me all the time?"

"Because you're my brother."

"Hmm. So that's your answer to everything. Tell me, why did the chicken cross the road?"

"Because it parked its car behind the bakery."

"Good. As long as *that's* not because I'm your brother. I don't want to be responsible for chickens crossing roads and parking cars."

The bell rang and Ms. Jackson told the class about Rachel's experiment. She had the whole class gather around her desk.

Tamika put raisins and cheese at the end of the maze. Andy opened the toolbox and took out Blue. Then he put the gerbil at the beginning of the maze.

"Go!" Rachel said, and clicked the stopwatch.

Blue twitched its nose. It smelled the raisins and cheese and tried to find its way through the maze. It bumped into the walls lots of times and made a few wrong turns. Then, at last, it found its way to FINISH.

Rachel clicked the stopwatch again and announced the time: "One minute and thirty-seven seconds."

Blue ate some raisins and cheese. Then Tamika held Blue while Red went through the maze. It took Red longer to get to FINISH. Rachel timed the two gerbils a few more times through the maze, and each time Blue was faster.

When they were done, Rachel stroked Blue's fur and said, "Good, Blue. You're the winner." Then she stroked Red's fur and said, "You're good, too."

"You touch them?" one of Rachel's classmates asked her.

"Sure I do," Rachel said. "Andy and Tamika taught me how to handle the gerbils. You have to be gentle and not make any loud noises, and most of all you have to be careful not to drop them."

Andy put Blue and Red into the toolbox again. Ms. Jackson thanked him and Tamika for coming to their class and helping. Rachel thanked them, too.

Andy took the toolbox, and he and Tamika returned to their class.

"That was a surprise," Andy told Tamika as they walked through the halls. "I didn't know Rachel likes me."

"But I did," Tamika said.

"I've been waiting for you," Ms. Roman said when they entered the class.

Andy wondered if he was in trouble again.

"I wanted you to be here when I discussed the stories you wrote yesterday." Ms. Roman took a pile of papers from her desk and said, "They are all very good."

Except mine, Andy thought.

"I'll read to you one that was especially well written. When I read it I identified with the main character in the story. It felt to me that *I* was in real trouble. The story is called, 'I'm a Criminal—Wanted by the Police.'"

"Hey, that's mine!" Andy called out.

"I know it's yours," Ms. Roman said. "And it's very well done."

"It is?"

Ms. Roman smiled and read Andy's story.

Rachel likes me, Andy thought. *Ms. Roman likes my story. This is the beginning of what might be a good day for me—a* really *good day.*

Andy listened as Ms. Roman read his story, and he thought, *Maybe from now on I'll be a great student, like Tamika and Stacy Ann Jackson. Maybe from now on, I'll have* only *good days.*

He listened some more, as Ms. Roman continued reading his story. *No,* he decided. *I'm still Andy Russell. I'll still get in lots of trouble, so I may as well enjoy today. Who knows when I'll have another good day?*

Bruce clapped when Ms. Roman finished reading Andy's story. Soon everyone in class was clapping. Andy stood and bowed.

Maybe I'll become a writer, Andy thought, *and write bestsellers and live in a great big house and be on television! Imagine that! Andy Russell, best-selling author!*

Andy imagined what it would be like to be a writer. He stood there and imagined owning a large boat and meeting the president.

"ANDY RUSSELL," Ms. Roman said, "are you planning to sit down?"

Andy looked at Ms. Roman. Then he looked at his classmates. *How long have I been standing here?* he wondered.

Andy quickly got in his seat. *I'm in trouble again,* he thought. *This good day didn't last long. It didn't even last one hour.*

Then Andy opened his notebook, looked at Ms. Roman, and pretended to listen to everything she said.

Turn the page for a sneak peek at Andy's next adventure....

So, Detective Andy Russell has solved another case, and now everything will get back to normal, right?

Well, not quite. In fact, *nothing* is normal in the Russell household! First, Andy's mother is rushed to the hospital to have her baby. Then, Tamika gets the news that her parents have recovered from their accident, and she can move back home with them!

It's time for lots of celebration—that is, until Andy's unsmiling, spinach-cooking, pet-hating aunt Janet comes to take care of him, Rachel, and Tamika while Mr. and Mrs. Russell are at the hospital. The weird food Aunt Janet cooks is bad enough, but when she tries to get rid of his pets to prepare for the baby's arrival, Andy has to take action . . . before it's too late!

Join Andy in all of his adventures! If you liked
Andy Russell, NOT Wanted by the Police, you'll enjoy
reading the other books in this exciting series about
Andy, his friends, and his never-ending escapades.